ISBN 978-1-332-19149-9
PIBN 10296140

This book is a reproduction of an important historical work. Forgotten Books uses
state-of-the-art technology to digitally reconstruct the work, preserving the original format
whilst repairing imperfections present in the aged copy. In rare cases, an imperfection in
the original, such as a blemish or missing page, may be replicated in our edition. We do,
however, repair the vast majority of imperfections successfully; any imperfections that
remain are intentionally left to preserve the state of such historical works.

# 1 MONTH OF
# FREE
# READING

## at
## www.ForgottenBooks.com

By purchasing this book you are eligible for one month membership to ForgottenBooks.com, giving you unlimited access to our entire collection of over 700,000 titles via our web site and mobile apps.

To claim your free month visit:
www.forgottenbooks.com/free296140

English
Français
Deutsche
Italiano
Español
Português

# www.forgottenbooks.com

**Mythology** Photography **Fiction**
Fishing Christianity **Art** Cooking
Essays Buddhism Freemasonry
Medicine **Biology** Music **Ancient
Egypt** Evolution Carpentry Physics
Dance Geology **Mathematics** Fitness
Shakespeare **Folklore** Yoga Marketing
**Confidence** Immortality Biographies
Poetry **Psychology** Witchcraft
Electronics Chemistry History **Law**
Accounting **Philosophy** Anthropology
Alchemy Drama Quantum Mechanics
Atheism Sexual Health **Ancient History**
**Entrepreneurship** Languages Sport
Paleontology Needlework Islam
**Metaphysics** Investment Archaeology
Parenting Statistics Criminology
**Motivational**

# Discovery of Natural Electricity.

THE first discovery of the Electric Currents in the stones and rocks at Hillman, Ga., was made by REV. A. L. HILLMAN, and that alone would have entitled him to honor and fame, but now that he has made another discovery equally important his name should be inscribed in bold letters on the roll of honor. He has discovered and given to the world two great remedial agencies, namely: Natural Electricity flowing from a large rock, and a water which prevents and cures sea-sickness, whereby it is believed more human suffering will be ameliorated than by any other discoveries in the history of the world.—THE SOUTH ATLANTIC.

# ROCKS THAT SHOCK;

OR, THE

Great Electrical Wonder at Hillman, Ga.

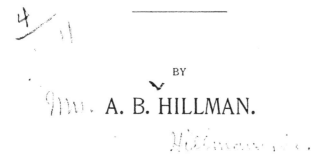

BY

Mrs. A. B. HILLMAN.

# ROCKS THAT SHOCK.

## CHAPTER I.

" To matter or to force
   The all is not confined ;
Besides the law of things
   Is set the law of mind.
One speaks in rock and star,
   And one within the brain—
In unison at times,
   And then apart again.
And both in one
   Has brought us hither,
That we may know
   *Our whence and whither.*"

"And both in one has brought us hither," we repeated, as we alighted from the carriage that brought us to the wonderful "rocks that shock," at Hillman, Georgia. These rocks produce shocks similar to a battery, and give the same tingling sensations. Patients or persons who receive these shocks by sitting or standing by the rock frequently tremble from head to foot as if they had no control of themselves. From these shocks many miraculous cures are made. Some are cured in a few hours, some in a day, while others it takes weeks, and even months, to cure. Altogether these rocks are a great curiosity as well as a mystery, and we have come to see this wonder, and if we get a shock will mention it further on.

The discoveries in the field of modern medical science have been so profound as to lead to mysticism. Dr. Koch and his lymph created a ripple that ran around the whole world, and, in New York, Dr. A. M. Phelps, professor of orthopedic surgery, in furnishing Johnny Githens with a firm shin-bone in place of an imperfect one, by substituting the bone taken from the leg of a little dog named Gyp for the bad one provided by nature for the lad Johnny, also caused a profound sensation.

But the great mystifier of the age is something that is commonly called electricity. It does not refuse to be bridled and made to work in harness, but there is yet to be found the scientist who can make plain the crooked paths of electricity so plain that the man who runs may read. And, again, it has a way of doing things of its own sweet will, the manner whereof passeth the ken of man. Electricity, for the present, seems destined to keep its secret of enormous transcendent value closely to itself, only giving to the world the bounteous benefits that it alone can give as the coming universal basis for the cure of nearly all ailments.

It was discovered thousands of years ago, and has been called by some, says Cobban, "an imponderable fluid." He prefers to call it "the spirit of life," and he further declares that the proper definition of electricity is "Energy," quoting from Arabian authority of ancient origin to prove this. "It flows and thrills in the nerves of men and women, animals and plants, throughout the whole of nature. It connects the entire round of Cosmos by one glowing, teasing, and agonizing principle of being, and makes us and beasts and trees and flowers all kindred!"

When the burden of life is made heavy by the loss of health and youth, and becomes intolerable, the victim naturally looks around for some fountain at which he can drink and have the ether of life and nervous force renewed. De Soto thought that the fountain of youth was in Florida. He made a close guess. It is hard by in Georgia.

Come, follow these lines, and they will show the Rocks that Shock and give you an imperfect idea, it is true, of their wonderful powers, but sufficient to enable you to form an estimate of their mysterious works.

## CHAPTER II.

In the fall of 1886 the newspapers began to talk of a Georgia wonder that had been accidentally discovered on his farm by Rev. Andrew L. Hillman. The remarkable cures that had been made created a sensation in the neighborhood, and notwithstanding Mr. Hillman made no effort to advertise the matter, the State press commented upon the strange discovery, and enterprising correspondents sent the item abroad over the wires to other papers.

The Richmond (Virginia) *Dispatch*, perhaps the most enterprising newspaper in the South, sent a special correspondent to the scene, with instructions to give the facts in the case. Here is what he wrote, and in this the story of the discovery of the rocks is told:

*A Wonderful Rock—Hillman's Electric Rock Down in Georgia—Its Discovery, and How its Natural Shocks Give Health to the Rheumatic and Dyspeptic.*

[Correspondence of the Richmond Dispatch.]

SHARON, GA., *February 25, 1887.*

The sudden stopping of the cars on the Atlantic Coast Line shook up the passengers at a wood and water station near Columbia, South Carolina.

It was midnight. Those who had been dissembling sleep straightened up, as did those who really had been snoozing. Some poked their heads out of the windows and looked up and down the road in the darkness.

" What place is this, sir ? "

" I do not know."

" What is the matter with that fellow yonder near the engine ? "

"Sick, I reckon; I saw him throwing up wood just now."

The drowsy monotone of voices inside the coach now sound clear and distinct, and in strange contrast to the clatter of the cars which so lately preceded it.

"Going down to Georgia, sir?"

"Yes."

"Far as Atlanta?"

"No; I stop at Sharon, on the Georgia railroad, and intend visiting Hillman's Electric Rock."

"Well, I have heard a great deal about the place, and I am booked for it myself, and I am glad I met you. I am from Elizabeth, New Jersey."

The train pulled out and the new acquaintances talked about the wonders of the Electric Rock.

### LOCATION OF THE ROCK.

Sharon was reached, and here the principal talk was about the Rock.

"Going to Hillman's Rock, sir?" is the first question you are asked, and you are importuned by colored drivers, who beg you, "Go wid me, boss."

The Georgia railroad is one of the most solid in the Union, the stock being worth $202. The Rock is on the Washington branch of this road, and is distant from Sharon about three miles. A siding has been built, and a depot is in process of erection. This depot is about half a mile from the Rock, which is in Taliaferro county, Georgia, seven miles from Crawfordville, the home of A. H. Stephens, and twelve from Washington, Georgia, where General Robert Toombs lived and died.

The plantation upon which the Rock is situated consists of 2,700 acres of very fine land, the property of Andrew L. Hillman, a Baptist minister, an active, energetic young man, who fitly represents the progressive spirit of the New South.

## HOW IT WAS DISCOVERED.

The history of the discovery of the great wonder (the like of which has never been known) is as follows:

Mr. Hillman is somewhat of a mineralogist, and for years has been sinking shafts in search of gold and alum on his place. Many of these attempts proved unsuccessful; but nothing daunted, in August, 1885, he commenced to sink a shaft at the foot of a mountain, the top of which, hundreds of feet above the Shaft, is capped with huge borders of rock that indicated the presence of alum. The ascent to the top of the mountain is precipitous, but, once reached, a commanding view of the country for miles around is presented, and a more pleasing one can hardly be found in any State.

## THE FIRST CURE.

At the time Hillman commenced his search for alum he was in bad health, but his energy did not desert him. He was suffering from severe rheumatism and dyspepsia, and in the hope that the exercise would relieve him he went into the shaft daily and worked an hour or so. A few feet from the surface a fine specimen of alum rock was found, and through this, with the aid of drill and blast, the work was pushed.

In handling the drill Hillman felt a peculiar sensation, similar to that experienced from a shock given by a galvanic battery. "Sometimes," said he, "the hands could hardly hold the drill. To my astonishment," he continued, "I found my dyspepsia greatly improved and my rheumatism completely gone. I persevered, and found myself restored to perfect health. I found water at the depth of fifteen feet, and cut under the mountain side of the Rock, at right angles, a square hole in the rock, as a receptacle for the water. I took a medical gentleman with me to get his opinion of the matter, but he did not give me any very great encouragement. I went to Atlanta in the spring of 1886, leaving the Shaft covered.

## CALLOWAY'S DELIGHT.

I returned in September, 1886, and again visited the Rock. The old ladder I had left in the well was almost rotten, but otherwise there was no difference in the looks of the place. I had been thinking a great deal about the curative properties of the place as shown in my own case, and I thought I would make other tests of it. A colored man named Charles Calloway had been suffering from severe rheumatism. His right arm was glued to his body, and he had no use of it. After a great deal of persuasion I induced him to go into the Shaft, and in ten days he was shoving a jack-plane. "There is the man now; ask him about it."

Calloway grinned from ear to ear as he spoke of the good the Rock had done him.

Similar cures of dread dyspepsia were also made. "The next man was Mr. John P. Moore, a thriving farmer of the neighborhood," said Mr. Hillman, "and he was cured completely. And then came Captain Joseph W. White, travelling passenger agent of the Georgia railroad. He was delighted with his relief from rheumatism. And later, Mr. A. P. Norman, assistant travelling agent, came down, and was made happy with the results of the visit."

### MISERABLE ACCOMMODATIONS.

The press took hold of the matter, and sufferers from various States came to see the wonderful electric cure. Accommodations were miserable in the neighborhood, but rheumatism and dyspepsia made sufferers more so, and people flocked to the place. Neuralgia, rheumatism, dyspepsia, and kidney troubles fled at the touch of electricity and the taste of the waters of the well. Mr. Hillman had made a discovery that baffled science. He saw that he had found what the world needed sadly. He wanted to shut down the Shaft until he could make it sightly and comfortable to visitors. The spot was picturesque enough—the mountain top, forest-crested, for the background; smiling meadows, green-clad; laughing streams, fringed with alders and willows, and undulating, changeable scenery, for the balance of the beautiful surroundings. The woods and meadows were vocal with the music of birds. Nature had blessed the spot, but there were the rude, unsightly shanties, hastily built, that put to the test faith in the virtues claimed for the place. Still the people poured in by hundreds—many out of curiosity, others for relief. The latter begged Hillman not to shut down, and declared that they were willing to put up with anything to be cured. He con-sented, determining to prosecute his improvement as best he could under the circumstances. A force of hands was at once put to work to enlarge the Shaft to such dimensions as would accommodate the people. A contract was made with the Schofield Brothers, the celebrated hotel men of Augusta. They will build a fine hotel on the mountain top, and prepare for the comfort of all who visit the Rock. The land adjacent to the hotel has been surveyed and laid off into lots, and it is no fool's guess that in a few years a thriving village will take the place of the tall foresters and bleak surround-ings there now.

## A VISIT TO THE ROCK.

The first time I saw the Rock was on a rainy morning last week. Near a rude frame shanty, under the tall trees of the swamp, miles from any other habitation, stood a number of vehicles. Several horses were tied to the swinging limbs of the trees. Men with that peculiar melancholy look that denotes suffering from protracted disease were standing in knots close by the shanty; others were inside sitting around a stove; a lady neatly-dressed stood in the doorway. A force of hands was digging with pick and spade a huge gap in the mountain side. The dew was glittering on the morning grass, and the mists were curling close to the tree-tops.

I went down a flight of steps and stood in the Shaft. Six men were sitting on splint-bottom chairs, silent and motionless. Four moist walls rose above them fifteen feet. The sides of these walls consisted of a curious-looking rock, a mixture of gray and red colors and an occasional vein of white. The light came dimly from above through panes of glass.

"Come down and take a seat, sir," said one of the men. I found my way to a seat and commenced to talk to the sufferers.

One of them, Mr. Hammonds, of Abbeville, S. C., could scarcely walk with the aid of crutches. He had suffered with rheumatism for fifteen years. Two days from the time I saw him he had thrown away his crutches and could leap nimbly from his buggy. This is only one of many cases of similar sort.

I had been in the Shaft but a short time before I felt the peculiar tingling sensations caused by electricity. My limbs began to shake and the perspiration to flow.

### THE TREATMENT, ETC.

I went out satisfied that there was something wonderful in the Rock, but I could not explain it.

As dark and dismal as the place is now, numbers of ladies and gentlemen spend the night at the Shaft, some of them sleeping in it, while the frogs pipe their spring love-songs and the hooting owl indulges in his idiotic laugh close by.

In course of time Hillman will be prepared to accommodate the public properly. Then he will be glad to see them. At present he tries to keep people away, but they come all the same.

Letters pour in to him from every State in the Union asking for particulars about this truly great Georgia wonder.     P. J. B.

It will be observed that the correspondent alluded to the damp and dismal nature of the surroundings. All of these have disappeared before the strides of improvement. The hand of magic has been at work, and of this work further on more will be said of a descriptive sort. Then, again, the correspondent called the place "a shaft," but as the force of imponderable fluid was given out by the rocks, visitors have given a more appropriate name—"Rocks that Shock."

## CHAPTER III.

The spirit of research and improvement has permeated the age and manifests itself in every phase of life. Anything unknown or undiscovered must forthwith be investigated by this practical generation. Accordingly, curious people with plenty of means went down to Mr. Hillman's Georgia farm to see for themselves the wonders of his electrical discovery. They were convinced that what had been said did not in any wise exaggerate facts. They found Mr. Hillman a quiet young Baptist minister, with a big plantation, and a plenty of this world's goods to satisfy his wants. He was generous, hospitable, and talked out freely. His mind was well stored with abundant information on other subjects as well as theology, and his visitors were well satisfied that the field for investment in these Rocks that Shocked with the unseen and subtle agency called electricity was full of promise of a rich reward.

A company was formed; a hotel of pleasing appearance and ample dimensions capped the summit of the mountain; close to the railroad a depot was erected, a post-office established, and the name "Hillman" given to the place, which now began to assume the airs of a village. Hillman was also the name given the post-office. The chain and compass of the civil engineer was called into use, and graded walks and roads swept in gentle circles around the mountain to the top of it. The axe was laid to such trees as marred the view, the marsh lands were drained, and a neat and commodious reception room built at the Rock. Visitors came in from the frozen regions of the North and West, and from all parts of the sunny South, and in all cases—even chronic ones of long standing—received substantial relief or permanent cure. Science so far has been unable to tell exactly what electricity is. The difficulties of ascertaining this are peculiarly intense, because the only testimony in regard to the phenomena in question has to be obtained from those who are, or have been, under its influence.

## "A GREAT MYSTERY."

The discovery so close to his doors of this Electric Rock provoked the following editorial from the pen of the great Georgia editor, Henry W. Grady, under the caption above given. He said:

"Electrical science is making wonderful progress, but no one has ever been able to tell just what electricity is, nor have its remarkable manifestations ever been explained.

"Every day we read of some odd development of this mysterious force. Now it is the electric girl in Georgia, who shocks everything that she touches; and, again, we have the astonished gentleman in Kentucky, who found upon stripping himself that he was a veritable pillar of flame, blazing up so brilliantly that he was able to read fine print by the light of his own countenance, to say nothing of the remainder of his *tout ensemble*, so to speak.

"We laugh at such freaks, and have our doubts, and yet there is nothing new in all this. In old times equally astonishing discoveries were made. Tiberius had a freedman who used an electrical fish to cure him of the gout. An ancient philosopher found that while he was undressing his body emitted crackling sparks and blazed out into a flame, after the fashion of the Kentuckian. For thousands of years people regarded electricity as a fantastic, uncertain, and amusing thing. Men played tricks with pieces of amber and glass tubes, and the Englishman who used to pull off his silk stockings to see them rush together when they were of different colors, and fly from each other when they were of the same color, was regarded as a very profound scientist.

"Century after century passed, and no successful attempt was made to utilize this powerful force. Men found out that it existed in their own bodies, in various objects, in the air and in the earth, but they did not know what to do with it. Within the past two generations we have made this tricksy spirit carry our messages, furnish our light, and move our machinery and railway trains; but we are merely at the beginning of our work. We know that this force can be made to serve us and destroy us. It will strike us dead, or it will cure us of our bodily ills. But, so far as understanding the mystery of it all is concerned, we are no better off than were the people thousands of years ago who were wondering at their snapping, crackling hair, and their luminous legs. It is about the biggest thing that we ever tackled, and in the course of time it is destined to do all of our work, except our brain work. But, after all, what is it?"

The editor of the *Constitution* followed this, after a visit to the Rock, with an editorial, which reads:

### "THE ELECTRICITY OF GEORGIA.

"The State of Georgia seems to take the lead in developing electric phenomena.

"Only a short time since Miss Lula Hurst startled the world with a wonderful and unexplained electric power that had been quietly developed in a peaceful Georgia home. She made money, and finally married and settled down to enjoy the fruits of electricity at the old homestead. The excitement about her wonderful power is still fresh in the recollection of our people, and another wonder in Georgia over electricity comes squarely before the public to be investigated and criticised.

"In Taliaferro county, between Barnett and Washington, about three miles from Sharon, on the west side of the Washington branch road and adjoining the railroad, is a large hill—they call it a mountain in the neighborhood. The owner of the land on this hill, in mining for alum a short time since, found on sinking a shaft about ten feet deep and eight feet in diameter, that there was a strong electric current given out on the surface of the pit next to the mountain. He also found that one of the laborers, who was afflicted with rheumatism when he commenced to excavate, had also recovered from his attack of rheumatism. He soon found other cases of rheumatism in this neighborhood and tried them in his new pit. They were speedily cured, and now everybody with rheumatism in the neighborhood and all over the State is flocking there to be cured. Fully half who go get relief, and there is, consequently, a sensation equal to the Lula Hurst excitement in store for this electric show. What affinity there is between alum rock and electricty we are unable to say, and how this wonderful current is stored in the ground to be used for a thousand purposes we cannot understand; but there it is without doubt, performing wonderful cures, even in its crude state—in the hands of men who are not at all skilled in its use—and ready at any moment to develop into something miraculous as soon as it can be trained by scientific hands.

"Cannot we find among the sons of Georgia one man who can explain these wonderful curiosities of nature in our State? Nature seems impatient at concealing them so long. They will be discovered and utilized, and the man who moves on these secrets first and utilizes them will be as great a hero in the future as Franklin and Morse."

The owner of the land mentioned is Rev. Andrew L. Hillman. He discovered the rock, named it the Electric Rock, is utilizing it, and no scientist so far has been able to contradict his theory by supplying a better name.

SEEING IS BELIEVING.

The Atlanta *Constitution* sent a special correspondent down to Hillman to write up the new discoveries. Here is what he published:

HILLMAN, GA., *March 17, 1888.*

" You cannot argue away these crutches, for here they are."

The speaker was Mr. Curley, of Rochester, New York. The place was perhaps the most remarkable spot in America.

Just view the scene: Three dry rooms, with the walls of rock and dirt exposed; around these walls long benches crowded with people holding their hands as if in pious exhortation against the dirt; some standing with their backs against the rock and their hands behind their coats, as a well-to-do man warms himself at a fire; some shaking as if in hysteria; some perfectly stiff, with an expression of inquiry on the face as if listening to distant thunder—all absorbed and in wrapt contemplation.

It is the Electric Rock of Georgia, or, we might say, the Electric Rock of the world, for there is no other. From the depths of this rock and dirt, is given out some quality—magnetism, electricity, mesmerism, or what not—that effects visibly about two-thirds of the people who lay their hands against it. It is said that during a thunder storm the face of this Rock is livid with lightning.

But, to go back to Mr. Curley. He says:

" I came here two weeks ago on those crutches. The visitors here know that I was barely able to drag myself on crutches from the carriage to the steps. I now walk with this slender cane with the slightest difficulty. I have no theory, but I have a fact. I had rheumatism when I came here; now I am going to leave without it."

" How did you happen to come? "

" I have had rheumatism for ten years. It has defied all treatment. I spent this winter in Cuba, where the atmostphere was dry and warm. I was leisurely making my way back North, and stopped in Augusta. I heard of this Electric Rock. I came here hobbling on crutches and tortured with pain. This afternoon I have walked about with you gentlemen, and none of you could tell that I ever had rheumatism. I am well."

Now, many of the wise physicians who heard this story declared that rheumatism cannot be cured in two weeks by any sort of medicine. The reply to this might be, that the Electric Rock is not medicine. Dr. Westmoreland, who was very much interested in the case, and who examined Mr. Curley thoroughly, insisted that he never had rheumatism, but that it was a nervous affection; to which Mr. Curley replied, that it had been a disabling and torturing misery for ten years, and that the best physicians in the North had pronounced it rheumatism, and that the Electric Rock had cured it. "However," he said, reflectively, "of course I do not blame the medical profession for doubting that a rock in the ground is better than a doctor."

### TESTING ITS POWER.

It is a queer thing to hear the patients talk. Man after man stands up and tells you that he came there absolutely disabled from rheumatism, and that he leaves there perfectly well. They seem to be satisfied to accept this fact, without trying to explain it, but faithfully stand by their works. Go to the Rock when you will, you will find them hugging the walls with the devotion of a saint against a shrine. All night long they will lay against the damp rock, and emerge from it when the sun clears the horizon.

A marked manifestation of the power of the electric room, whether imaginary or real, was furnished by two ladies. They were of high character and intelligence. Upon placing their hands against the wall their pulse accelerated, their hands trembled until in a few moments the quiver ran up the arms, and extended through the body. Then they shook uncontrollably, every nerve and every muscle quivering until it was almost painful to see them. Physician after physician took hold of their hands, held their shoulders, and attempted to control them, but fifty men could not have stilled that unaccountable quivering and shaking. They finally left the wall and were taken into the upper pavillion, and the physicians took hold of their hands again and tried to quiet them, but without avail. Dr. Devine stated that the pupil of the eye of one of them failed to respond to the light when turned towards it. Each of the ladies answered questions in a hurried sort of voice, tremulous with emotion, and there was neither cessation or relief until they had fallen asleep and slept it off as they would have done with a powerful medicine.

What was it? Hysteria, some of the physicians said. Perhaps it was, but it was produced whenever they put their hands against the wall, and it subsided just when the body, apparently charged with electricity, had apparently regained equilibrium.

On one of the benches in one of the apartments sat an intelligent young man, who watched the proceedings with interest. It was Mr. McCall, editor of the Union Spring *Herald*, in Alabama. Mr. McCall had no theory about the Rock, but he had a fact. "I came here," he said, "eight days ago, bent up with rheumatism. I am going to leave here to-morrow for my home perfectly well. I cannot explain it, but I know it."

Mr. McCall stated that on the first of the year he was invited to a leap year ball. He was getting ready for it when he was seized with reumatism in his knees and his elbows. This clearly incapacitated him for participation in the festivities. The rheumatism in his elbows would prevent his holding his partner in the dance, while the rheumatism in his knees would have prevented him threading with her the mazy waves of the waltz. He, therefore—properly, we think—staid at home. "From that time forward I was the victim of rheumatism," said Mr. McCall. "I could not attend to my business, and I was in constant pain. I had the best physicians I could get. I finally read about the Electric Rock in the *Constitution*, and made up my mind to try it.

### CONVINCED BEYOND CAVIL.

"My friends laughed at the idea, but I came ahead, and I am cured. I do not know what cured me, but here I am," and with a vigorous swing of his arms and a gentle pirouette of his legs, Mr. McCall gave evidence that he was on deck for the next leap-year ball.

"For the first day," he said, "after getting here I felt nothing. I stayed in the room all day, and pretty much all night, and beyond a little tingling sensation now and then there was nothing. But I thought I would try it another day. The next day my pain decreased. I would frequently sit six hours in the room without moving, either reading or writing, and in a week I was perfectly free from pain, and, I believe, permanently cured of rheumatism. At first I was discouraged. It appeared to me that a well man would catch rheumatism by sitting in there, but I have seen the most delicate ladies, who would not dare to get their feet damp, come and sit here by the hour in all sorts of weather, and I have never heard of one catching cold yet. On the contrary, it is the almost universal testimony that there is a glow about the feet, and a considerable warming up of the body, the longer one sits here. This applies in winter as well as summer."

Many people are not affected at all by the Rock. They go in as skeptics, and come out confirmed in their skepticism. No one knows what the power of the Rock is. Many scientific men pronounce it chimerical to talk about it; but there are cures. All the science in America, for instance, cannot convince Mr. McCall, of the Union Springs *Herald*, that the Electric Rock cannot cure rheumatism, for the simple reason that it did cure Mr. McCall.

### VISITORS HERE.

Colonel C. H. Phinizy, president of the Georgia railroad, went up from Augusta in his private car with his wife, Major John W. Green and wife, Colonel and Mrs. J. W. White, Mr. T. R. Gibson, Miss Lillie White, Dr. Eugene Foster, Dr. W. H. Dougherty, Jr., and Mr. T. P. Henry. Colonel P. Walsh came up on a later train.

Washington's delegation was: Mr. J. A. Benson, Mr. R. T. Du Bose, Mr. William M. Sims, Hon. F. H. Colley, Mr. Thomas C. Hogue, Miss Nora Palmer, Miss Mary Hardeman, Hon. M. P. Reese, Rev. J. E. Hammond, and Messrs. W. C. Cade, William H. Anthony, N. H. Pope, T. Burwell Green, and G. W. Mulligan.

The Atlanta party was composed of the following ladies and gentlemen: Captain and Mrs. Evan P. Howell and daughter, Mr. Henry W. Grady, ex-Governor R. B. Bullock, Dr. Willis F. Westmoreland, Mr. G. H. Vining (of the *Evening Capitol*), Dr. T. S. Powell, Dr. E. J. Roach, Dr. C. A. Stiles, Dr. P. E. Murry, Dr. John Z. Lawshe, Dr. K. C. Devine, Dr. W. A. Crow, Dr. Willis B. Parks, Dr. H. F. Scott, Dr. A. G. Thomas, Dr. J. C. Avery, Dr. W. M. Durham, Dr. F. H. O'Brien, and Messrs. W. J. Cole, J. A. McDonald, and Dr. S. T. Biggers.

From Athens: Prof. and Mrs. H. C. White, Mr. Samuel C. Benedict, Mrs. C. D. Flanigan, and Messrs. E. D. Stone, J. S. K. Axson, and Albert Howell, Jr.

The other guests were: Messrs. F. M. Delano and J. L. Carleton, of New York; Dr. R. C. Word, of Decatur; Dr. B. B. Lenoir, of Lenoir, Tenn.; Mr. and Mrs. O. F. Bane, of Chicago; Dr. J. W. Bailey, of Gainesville; Mr. W. F. Kenfield, of San Francisco, and Messrs. M. G. Sharon and J. G. Wright, of Ragtown.

### TO BE THOROUGHLY TESTED.

Of course it was not possible in the short time for the visitors on this trip to give an accurate opinion about the effect of the resort on certain diseases. It was not intended for that, but simply to draw the attention of the scientific and medical men in this State to what was there and its results. Messrs. Delano, Carleton, and Cole, the electricians of the party, will, as soon as possible, procure a galvanic meter and make a thorough test of the electric qualities of the place. The proprietors, we are informed, will ask the Georgia Medical Association, at its annual meeting in May at Rome, to appoint a committee of leading physicians to make a thorough test of the benefits claimed, and that this committee be empowered to see what, if any, remedy there is for any of the various diseases claimed to be cured. They claim that there have been many wonderful cures of nervous diseases. They claim further, that many persons who go there with a normal pulse, say seventy-eight or eighty, after being in there for a short time, without any exertion, will find their pulse go up to one hundred and two and one hundred and four, or even higher sometimes, and in other cases the reverse will occur. In some cases there will be a perceptible shaking of the whole person, and in others it will not be felt. As Colonel Ben C. Yancey, who is there with his wife, spending a week, says: "There is some kind of force there, and it is unknown, and the scientific and medical men ought to be able to work it out. I cannot," says Colonel Yancey, "say whether it is electricity or what it is, because I do not know. This much I can say, there is some unknown force displayed there, and it is an interesting chapter, in my opinion, for scientific men to explain."

Dr. B. B. Lenoir, of Lenoir, Tenn., is there, and will remain over for a week. Miss Millie Rutherford, with her mother, Mrs. William Rutherford, was there last week, and returned home Saturday. Several of the physicians will make further test by sending patients they think will be benefited.

# CHAPTER IV.

*A Second Visit to Hillman, Georgia—A Double Attraction at the Place.*

Quite a year has passed since our first visit to Hillman, and, as we expected, found the place greatly improved. But the greatest attraction we found was Mr. Hillman's latest discovery of another

## GRAND ELECTRIC ROCK

on the south side of the Electric Mountain. Since his discovery of the first rock he has been closely inspecting the surroundings of this marvellous place, and finding an immense rock a quarter of an acre long, containing the same mineral, he engaged a prospector, a miner, and some workmen, and commenced an excavation on the south side of the rock. After cutting some three or four feet into the rock the miner seated himself to make an experiment, and was so severely shocked he called to the workmen to come and help him out, and the man who took hold of his hands to help him out received a severe shock also.

Then Mr. Hillman was thoroughly convinced of the true virtue of this Rock. He then continued the excavation until he got it about a medium size room. All the time the men were working in it they would get so full of electricity they would have to go out and a new set go in, thus alternating until completed. Then carpenters finished up the whole with the needed wood work, such as floors, windows, doors, reception room, and a neat little porch. It was very noticeable that all the men who worked in and about this

Rock greatly improved in health and had enormous appetites, and said they felt so strong and active they wanted to sing and dance.

Visitors from the north Electric Rock and the hotel would flock around to see the new great wonder, often asking Mr. Hillman for some of the rock chipped from the excavation. They would say, as they held the pieces in their hands, "Oh, I can feel it; I can feel the electricity even in this piece of rock. Do let us carry some home"—which many did.

Mrs. S. M. Dawson, the lovely wife of the lamented Captain Dawson, of Charleston, South Carolina, came to Hillman for treatment, accompanied by her son Warrenton. She came around to the south side Rock during its excavation, and Mr. Hillman gave her some of the rocklets. As she held them in her hand she exclaimed, "Oh, what a treasure; I can feel the electricity so acutely in these little rocks. What a power that large one must be."

She carried them home, and soon after made a visit to New York, taking them with her. She wrote Mr. Hillman that her New York friends were greatly enthused over the little electric rocks she carried from Hillman, and that they had begged every one of them from her. Mrs. Dawson was interviewed by a reporter of the Charleston *News and Courier*. She told him the great virtue in this rock was beyond the comprehension of scientific men, and that marvellous things would be heard from it.

Visitors and patients were anxious to see this second wonder completed and the room ready to seat patients; and when Mr. Hillman was ready to receive the patients, the patients were ready to receive the electricity, and it was wonderful to see the effect it had on them. Sometimes very excitable scenes would take place. Some patients would have to be taken out on account of becoming overcharged;

some would be so pleasantly shocked they would be laughing, while with others it was the great expectation of getting a *big shock.*

We remember several of them, which we will mention, to show the peculiarity of cases. One of the overcharged patients was Miss Fannie Pouser, of South Carolina. She was quite an invalid, and was reclining on a cot in the electric room. Several patients were in the room at the same time, among them Mrs. Summerall, of Augusta, who was engaged in pleasant conversation with Miss Fannie. They had been talking some time when Mrs. Summerall noticed that Miss Pouser did not reply; she hastened to her and found the young lady unconscious. Some gentlemen took her up, cot and all, and ran out of the room, when she soon revived, and was so pleased to know she had at last received a shock. She had been a patient for two weeks and had so often wished for a shock, believing it would benefit her so much, and it really did.

Another patient who created quite an excitement from becoming overcharged was Mr. B. F. Cannon, of Alabama. He was a wreck from rheumatism, and unable to walk, but hopeful of recovery. He took the electricity well, and was finally overcharged and unconscious for half an hour, and afterwards when he felt the shock coming on he would tell the porter George to take him out. He would send George to the post-office every day for his mail, but after being overcharged he would always say, "Don't go and leave me in here, George; lift me into the sitting-room until you return." The strangest part about these shocks is, the patients crave them, and they always get better after getting them; and those who wait on Dr. Rock (as they sometimes call the Electric Rock), and fail to get a. shock, would not fail to worry and fret, and woe to the discoverer at such times because he did not discover a " *Lightning* rock that would flash the lightning into" them at once. Yet many take it so gradually they get well and never get the shock, and often get well after getting home.

We might as well tell of our experience, too, and test of this south side Rock: We were seated in the electric-room in a lively conversation with some ladies, when all at once we felt ourselves shaking without the least effort on our part. We looked around, and asked who was shaking the floor? No one, they all replied. Well, what is the matter with us? we asked. Oh, you are having a shock, they exclaimed, greatly amused at our bewilderment. We quickly left the room, feeling as light as air, and went out and stayed awhile, or until the sensation left us; and on returning, the identical influence would take hold of us again; so we sat in the doorway of the electric-room and continued our chat.

We had another experience with this *same Rock*. We had been suffering for several weeks with rheumatism. We took two hours' treatment by standing by the Rock one hour each day for two consecutive days, and we were cured.

This made a much deeper impression on us than to see others cured, for no one can conceive the remarkable relief but the suffering individual who gives this mystery a personal test.

We will mention the case of Mrs. Verderey, a charming lady from the sand hills of Augusta: She came with her husband and mother, and had scarcely been in the electric-room half an hour before she was in a perfect tremor from head to foot. She trembled and shook so severely that her husband and mother became alarmed, but after leaving the room for a short while the shock soon left her.

An amusing case of a young man was told to us by some of the patients. He was a gay young fellow, and came in and asked what he must do to get a shock. Put your hands on the Rock, said an old gentleman. All right; I want a shock; I want to know how it feels. He stood by the Rock and placed his hands on it, and pretty soon he knew how it felt, and also how he felt. He sprang away from the Rock and made for the door, and could not be induced to return.

Why is this Rock so powerful? is often asked of Mr. Hillman, and his supposition is, that being on the south side of the mountain the hot rays of the sun aid in generating electricity.

Further on in these notes we will mention some remarkable cures made in this south-side electric-room. As we have said, this Rock is a quarter of an acre long, very tall, and immense. It lies at the foot of the mountain, with lovely scenery all around. The north electric rock is a pretty place also, and has often been described by other writers.

# CHAPTER V.

On this south side of the mountain Mr. Hillman made two other very remarkable discoveries. One is the Magic Well; the other is the Nausea-Cure Spring. The magic water has derived its name from the magical effects it has on curing the worst cases of dyspepsia and indigestion.

The Nausea-Cure Spring is a great wonder. It is a specific for nausea, but the patient has to take it in small doses, or it will produce nausea. As the homœopathists say, *similia similibus curantur.* It cures cholera morbus, cholera infantum, and other ailments, and is a fine table water also.

Knowing this water was so fine for nausea, Mr. Hillman conceived the idea that it would also cure seasickness, and prevailed on several distinguished families and physicians to test it on the ocean, which they did with great success for seasickness.

This spring has been capitalized at $150,000, a company organized, with Dr. J. E. Green, of Augusta, Ga., president; Major Wm. Gary, Rev. A. L. Hillman, C. W. Conway, and others, stockholders. The place is becoming very famous, and we see many people here from far and from near, and nowhere have we ever seen strangers so kindly disposed. Each seemed to vie with the other in courtesy and kindness, in sympathy and soothing words. It must be that "fellow suffering made them wonderous kind."

Some of the patients said they really believed there was some magical influence around the place, or in the Electric Rock, that brought about such kind and pleasant sociability. Be that as it may, we have always found nice, agreeable visitors at this "unique resort." We say unique, because it really seems that this place is without a parallel. · We have heard it said that nature provides a remedy for every ailment of Adam's race, and that we will, sooner or later, find it if we search for it, and it really seems that Mr. Hillman has been guided by providence to find it at this place—for a great many, at least.

Many different experiences were told us, and as we recall some of them to mind, we think them worth relating.

A very wealthy lady was seated in the electric-room, and during a pleasant conversation with her she said: I was at the Hot Springs, Arkansas, some time ago for my health, and while taking one of those "hot baths" the nurse allowed me to remain in the bath a few minutes too long, which threw me into a congested state, and caused my circulation to be so sluggish that I suffer all the time with cold feet and hands, and nothing else relieves me like the treatment taken at this Electric Rock. After being here several days my feet and hands become warm and the circulation is so much better that it it improves my health generally. When my physician finds he cannot relieve me he tells me to go to Hillman; that there is something there that benefits me more than he can.

Another experience was a minister's daughter, who said when she arrived at the Electric Rock that her case was considered almost hopeless by her friends, and even her father despaired of her ever getting well. But, said she, I am so much better. The swelling has gone down, caused from liver trouble, and now I can lie on my back and sleep so sweetly all night; and I am so much stronger I can walk up this mountain.

A gentleman from Alabama was the next. He had been an invalid for nineteen years, suffering excruciating pain all the time from rheumatism, but he was a patient sufferer and devout Christian, who took his affliction so resignedly we could only think nothing but the grace of God enabled him to stand it so well. In speaking of his affliction he said: Through many trials, tribulations, and suffering we are called before we can gain an entrance into the "Kingdom of kingdoms." He seemed never to doubt his recovery, as he sat day after day in the electric-room, and at times becoming overcharged with electricity would have to be taken out and brought back alternately, until he was fully charged with the virtue of the Rock. In nine weeks he returned home, free from pain, and his general health greatly improved.

Mr. McLaughlen, of South Carolina, a very excellent gentleman, was also a patient with a severe case of rheumatism in his chest and shoulders, and had previously been so ill he had to be taken to Florida on a bed. He recovered sufficiently to attend to his business in the bank, but never well of rheumatism till he took treatment in the electric-room. His sister was with him at the same time, suffering with "compressed nerves of the ankles for twenty years." She was cured, and said that alone rewarded her for her visit to the Electric Rock.

We met Mr. Hawkins, of Beach Island, S. C. He went into the electric-room, and in less than ten minutes he was so affected by the electricity that he had to come out immediately. In about two hours he went back, and stayed fifteen minutes. We saw him coming out with a flushed face and in a profuse perspiration, saying he felt decidedly better. He came for nervous treatment; said his nerves were in an awful shattered condition. After remaining several days he felt greatly restored and much benefited.

And here, too, was Mrs. Dr. George, from Enterprise, Mississippi. She said her health was altogether broken down, and she was confined to her bed. Her husband had concluded to send her to the Hot Springs, Arkansas. She had her trunks packed to leave for that place, when one of her sons came home and told her he had met with a patient from the Electric Rock who had been cured there, and who spoke in the highest praise of its virtues. He advised her to go to the Rock. So, in company with one of her sons, she visited the Electric Rock, and, said she, I am so glad I came here. I like so much, and I feel so much better. In a few days we saw her again proudly walking down the steps into the electric-room without assistance, saying, "Oh, how glad I am that I can help myself." She was wonderfully benefited, and was delighted at her great improvement.

The case of a gentleman from Augusta, Georgia, was still more wonderful. He was confined to his bed with a severe case of rheumatism, and tortured with the most racking pains. The first day he was brought to the Rock he was considerably benefited, and could walk on his crutches. The second day he was so much better he could walk a short distance without them, and the third day we saw him get out of the phaeton and walk into the house as well as ever. This gentleman was one of those who take the electricity quickly and successfully—consequently made a rapid cure; while others take it slowly but surely, and in due course of time make fine cures.

We were so much pleased with pretty Mrs. Porter, from Florida, a quiet, dignified lady, and a great sufferer, like many of her sex.

She looked so sad and despairing when she came; so glad and rejoicing when she left. She told us she had been so wonderfully relieved that she wept tears of joy at her miraculous restoration.

Another lady as lovely as she—Mrs. Dillon, from Thomasville—suffered similarly, and told us she had not walked for years. She could walk very well when she left the Rock, and was much improved in health.

This wonderful Electric Rock has called forth a great deal of comment from learned and scientific men, and they seem more or less in the dark regarding its curative or remedial agencies, while all agree it is the work of nature, and wish to get at it in a more tangible form.

We quote Tyndall as saying: "Science ought to teach us to see the invisible as well as the visible in nature; to picture to our mind's eye those operations that entirely elude the eye of the body; to look at the very atoms of nature in motion and in rest, and follow them forth into the world of senses."

Emerson says: "Nature is a reservoir of power. Tremendous forces are all about us, but they are not adopted to our use."

Another writer says: "The forces of nature are strangely linked with our lives. Everywhere a Divine hand is developing ideas tenderly and wonderously related to human needs."

To the thoughtful mind all phenomena have a hidden meaning. It is the invisible nature of this Rock that mystifies one so. We walk into the electric-room and look around, wishing to see and know what is in this Rock that affords some such relief. All have similar ideas. It is amusing to see strangers come in the electric-room and look around and up at the rock wall. They almost feel alarmed, saying: "Will it knock me down if I put my hand on it ? " Some seem to think they might be shocked as if by lightning.

Many enjoy the new departure of pills, powders, and patent medicines, and to leave at home the miniature drugstore for the easy and effective remedy of nature. If one would wait on nature more, and assist it with some simple home remedy, it would save many a sick spell and dear doctor's fee.

Many of the patients at the Electric Rock said they had spent nearly all they possessed on the doctors, and when their skill was exhausted they would kindly advise them to go to the Electric Rock.

One lady we saw from Chicago said she had spent thousands of dollars on the doctors, gaining but little relief from her painful malady—sciatica. She is still very wealthy, her husband being a millionaire, and owning an immense mine in Georgia. He sent her to give the Electric Rock a trial. She had no relief from pain day or night, and often through the night would scream in agony from pains in her limbs. She came, and, greatly to her surprise and delight, she was soon so benefited that she could rest well at night, and only once during her stay did she have any symptom of the pains. When she left she spoke in the highest terms of the curative powers of the Electric Rock and her pleasant sojourn at Hillman.

A good many doctors have visited the Electric Rock for their own personal benefit, and some of them are nature's noblemen—good, strong-minded men. Often they were much benefited, and did not hesitate to give the Rock due credit for their improvement. Ah, we wish it could have done more for these good men—made them young again. It is so sad to see them growing old and feeble in their noble work of serving the sick.

Mr. Finney, from Jones county, Georgia, told us he came with a fearful headache. Said he: "My head has hurt me so much l am nearly deaf." "Are you any better?" we asked. "Oh, yes; my head is quite easy now, and I feel quite improved, though I have not felt the electricity, that I know of; but something has helped me." "You took it, then, and, like many others, was not aware of it," we replied." "Yes; I guess so," and continued he, "I have great faith in it. My wife was down here last year, and was shocked every time she put her hand on the rock wall, and would be thrown in a perfect quiver. She carried some of the rock dug out of the electric room with her home, and although it has been a year since she did it, it will shock her now when she takes it in her hand, and set her to trembling and shaking at once, while I can't feel it at all. We must be very differently constituted. It is a mystery to me that both of us should be so benefitted and our experience so dissimilar." We told him that it was nothing new to us. We knew of many such cases at this most singular of places.

One of the most wonderful cases that came under our observation was that of an old colored man, Wiley, whom the doctors pronounced physically sound. He has lived on the Hillman farm for twenty-odd years, and still lives in a few hundred yards of the Electric Rock. It has a powerful effect on him when he merely enters the electric-room, shaking him up to such an extent that he is sore for several days after.

On one occasion Dr. Sheppard, of Cincinnati, Ohio, timed him by his watch. He was in the electric-room one minute, when he asked to be taken out. They quickly helped him out, and he shook and trembled for several hours after. The Doctor examined him, and said if he were to remain in the electric-room long enough it would kill him, so well does the electricity take to him. He is very much opposed to going in again, and it would take a right good sum to tempt the old man to repeat it, for he says: " I is got no rheumatiz, an' I ain't gwine in dar for dat thing to git holt a me; nor I ain't." His case is a rare one, though, and we don't know whether he is full of electricity- or devoid of it.

A lady from South Carolina came to the Rock for treatment. She was badly afflicted with rheumatism. She took the electricity so well that in a few days she was well enough to return home. Her friends met her at the depot with a carriage. She informed them that she could walk, and to their utter astonishment she stepped out of the train and walked with perfect ease to her residence.

Prof. J. R. Blake, Sr., of Greenwood, S. C., recently visited the resort, and gives the result of his observations in the following extract from the Greenwood *Tribune:*

" The curative value of the place for some diseases is very remarkable. Rheumatism, dyspepsia, paralysis, and some forms of nervousness, were signally relieved in individuals coming under my personal observation. One young man from McCormick, S. C., who had been prostrated for seventeen months by deranged digestion, was cured thoroughly, gaining eighteen pounds in a month. An elderly gentleman from Penfield, Ga., who had been partially paralyzed on one side for eight years, arrived at the Rock in the same hack with myself. His right hand was disabled, and he walked with great difficulty when he arrived, but after six days in the electric-room could write letters to his family, and he walked with comparative ease about the grounds. Many such cases are reported by reliable persons familiar with the history of the place.

" Now, as to the remedial agencies at work in effecting these wonderful cures, I must speak with more caution. A very common impression prevailing at a distance is that the relief afforded partakes of the nature of the "faith cures," of which we hear so much; but no one can remain long at the place without being convinced that this hypothesis is indefensible. The prevailing theory among the visitors at the Rock is that the effect is produced from electricity derived from the walls and floor of the room. To test this belief in some practical form, I made the following experiment: Two No. 16 copper wires, each twelve feet long, were inserted into the walls at opposite corners of the shaft. In the absence of a scientific galvanometer, I introduced into the circuit of these wires several of the most equable and self-poised patients who were present, to see if they could detect any current from the wall through the wires. Six persons were introduced in succession, and all except one claimed to feel in the wires the same tingling sensations which they derived directly from the wall. Of course, excited imagination and nervous irritability are unknown quantities which cannot be eliminated from this problem so long as the human system is employed in its solution, but it is scarcely creditable that so many reliable and sober persons would be mistaken in identifying the sensation derived from the wires with the sensation given by the walls.

"There is much difficulty still remaining in this problem as to the origin of the electricity, the irregular, fitful way in which it acts, and many other points suggested by the abnormal conditions of the case."

ABOUT DYNAMOS—IS EQUALLY APPLICABLE TO THE "ROCKS THAT SHOCK."

Electric-light men are never troubled with rheumatism, says a local paper. The stiff-jointed portion of humanity hover around the big dynamos in the Brush light company's works just like consumptives seek a slaughter-house for the blood of a freshly-killed bullock. "Why, people would be lying around our dynamos all day if we permitted it," said Superintendent Law. The discussion upon the subject of electricity as a curative agent in certain chronic cases—notably rheumatism—has excited much interest among electricians and all classes of workmen engaged in handling heavily charged wires. Numerous cases are cited in different parts of the country to prove that men engaged in these employments are free from all rheumatic and neuralgic troubles. This appears to be the case in Philadelphia also.

Superintendent Law is ready to debate the question with the best informed doctor in the land. Eight years ago, when he first began to work around dynamos in San Francisco, he was afflicted with acute rheumatism. His fingers were twisted out of all natural shape and proportion by the insidious disease, and the joints were swollen to many times their natural size. His shoulders, hips, and knees were similarly affected, and he was, as he expressed it himself, so stiff that he could scarcely move. He soon began to improve, however, when he came in close contact with the dynamos, and although he was not cured immediately, his recovery was sure and rapid, and in less than eighteen months he was apparently a well man. He has had no recurrence of the trouble, and is convinced that the cure can be credited to nothing but the wonderful influence of the strong current of electricity with which he has constantly been surrounded for years.

Mr. Law speaks of a portion of his experience as rather in the nature of heroic treatment. He has been knocked down time out of mind by coming in contact, either through his own carelessness or by accident, with two wires, and on one occasion remained unconscious for ten minutes. The shock upon that occasion, he says, felt to him as though he had been hit in the neck by a sand bag. He was rather surprised to find himself still alive when he came to his senses. If life could be taken in that way, Mr. Law thinks it would be the most humane method of executing criminals. He suffered no pain from the shock except when he was burned, but he thinks it effectually banished the rheumatism.—*Electrical World.*

# CHAPTER VI.

## A Third Visit to Hillman, Ga.

We left Richmond, Va., several days before the holidays. We came on the Coast Line, much to our discomfort, for our Northern brethren were ahead of us and engaged every section in the sleepers, and we had to travel all night as best we could—now and then napping on our seat. The crow of the chicken cock at Florence had an unusual cheery sound, for we knew with the rising sun we would be nearing the good city of Augusta, where we would give up the tiresome seat of the railroad car for more comfortable quarters.

It is a noticeable fact that the Coast Line seems to be a favorite route for Northerners coming South for the winter. We chatted with some on this trip, and found them pleasant and communicative. A nice-looking old lady from Saratoga, N. Y., told me that she and her husband had been spending their winters in Florida for the last twenty-one years. She told us a good many were on the same train then bound for Florida. Another lady, from Jersey City, said she was then recovering from a prolonged attack of La Grippe, and fearing consumption would follow, her physician advised her to go South, as he had been cured by spending several months at Aiken, S. C. A gentleman said he had been cured of throat trouble by spending the winter in Augusta, Ga. Another said since he had made his home in the South he had recovered from asthma and other throat troubles. Some affirm that the fragrant odor of the piney groves in the South, and the use of the needle or straw that grows on the pine tree, was a great aid in their recovery from pulmonary troubles by sleeping on pillows stuffed with the pine needles. These Southern pines emit a most pleasant odor, which is more and more powerful as the summer advances, and is delightful to most people. We heard a very effusive and affectionate expression from a distinguished lady of Chattanooga, while riding through a pretty piney grove at Hillman. She said: Ob, these delightful pines; how I do love them. I feel as if I could caress every one of them.

We reached Augusta in due time, and after refreshments and a short rest seated ourselves in the nice coach of the popular Georgia railroad, and soon arrived at Hillman, where we anticipated spending the holidays. We found some pleasant parties at the hotel with the same intention: a gentleman, with his whole family, from Boston, some from Michigan, New York, Pennsylvania, Virginia, the Carolinas, and Tennessee. We found others than invalids enjoying the peculiarities of Hillman. The climate is mild and bracing in winter; cool and breezy in summer.

They say no blizzards or cyclones has ever yet touched the tops of these majestic hills, whose elevation is such that the lights of two cities (Washington and Sharon) can be seen in the distance. We will mention these towns later on, and return to the hotel and guests.

The hotel is a forty-four-room house, modern in its construction and conveniences; electric bell in each room; open fire-places and wood fires; bath rooms on each floor, provided with hot and cold water. In addition to several mineral waters, they have an abundant supply of freestone water. The hotel is on an elevation of 600 feet above the sea level, and the following as to temperature is taken from the United States Meteorological Records of the Smithsonian Institute, Washington, D. C.:

43

| Mean temperature, for 15 successive years, for Spring months | . . . . . . | 61.15 |
|---|---|---|
| "          "          "          "          " Summer " | . . . . . . | 75.74 |
| "          "          "          "          " Autumn " | . . . . . . | 60.77 |
| "          Winter " | . . . . . . | 46.06 |

We liked the family from Boston, and were glad to see the invalid daughter rapidly recovering from rhumatism and heart trouble.

Her parents said she could not stand the snows of the North; that whenever it snowed she suffered more intensely. They were also alarmed about her heart, as five home physicians had pronounced her heart organically diseased. But after remaining at Hillman five or six weeks, the heart trouble, as well as the rhumatism, seemed cured. The Hillman doctor disagreed with the Boston doctors in regard to its being a case of organic heart disease, as she could take rapid exercise up and down the mountain avenue, after a few weeks' stay, with ease and comfort. Several cases similar to this have been reported here, which proves not to be *heart* disease, but the national disease—dyspepsia.

Another case of interest to us was that of a delicate widow lady, who told us she had witnessed a cyclone in the South, and before she recovered entirely from its effect she witnessed another at the North, which brought on nervous prostration. She improved greatly, and was delighted with the "Rocks that Shock."

We found our hostess busy preparing for Christmas, and the young ladies from Boston assisting her in turning out handsome embossed cakes, home-made candies, and other delicacies of the season. But what we enjoyed most was the nice brown turkey, home-made sausage, and the fresh country butter and vegetables brought in by the country neighbors, who find a ready market for their merchandise at Hillman.

One of the most striking cases we saw here was Mrs. C. and her wonderful susceptibility to electricity. It was mainly her great enthusiasm over the Electric Rock that caused her husband to sell out and come to Hillman to reside, knowing the place was a perfect panacea for all the ills of his wife.

First, she was confined to her room from nervous prostration, brought on by a severe burn. She was not able to walk one step when she was brought to Hillman, and after a few days' treatment in the electric-room she could walk as well as ever, and remained well and hearty for twelve months, when a similar accident occurred (a scald from hot coffee on her arm at the breakfast table). Again she was prostrated, and had to be brought to Hillman, with the same happy results. She had scarcely been at Hillman a year when she sustained severe injuries from a railroad wreck, and was not able to move herself in bed. She was carried to the electric-room, and in one day's treatment (which is nothing but sitting or lying on a cot in the electric room) she was fully restored. She told us with tears in her eyes how grateful she was to her Heavenly Father for such a blessing as the Electric Rock.

We spent the holidays here very pleasantly, and meanwhile we were quite diverted in witnessing the quaint way the colored people of the far South have of celebrating the Christmas holidays on the great cotton plantations.

Mr. Hillman's farm consists of about twenty-five hundred acres of fertile and well-timbered land. He has a number of tenants, or croppers, as they are called here, all in comfortable quarters. They all called him "boss," from the oldest to the youngest. The old heads whom we saw here this winter of 1890 keep up their style of calling on the "Boss" every first day of Christmas with their kindly greetings and compliments of the season. One old fellow, who has lived with the Boss for many years, called to have his say: "De Lord is done spared us to see another Christmas day, Boss, and we done see de ole year most out. May we all live through de one dat is comin' in, an' many mo'; an' when we come to lay down an' die, we will fole our arms 'cross our peaceful breast, an' go home to dat shinnin' globe whar we trust we will lib forever."

They seem mostly to enjoy Christmas in rather a religious way. Some sit up Christmas-Eve night and watch for the dawn of Christmas day, and also watch the old year out and the new one in with singing and prayer. A quartette came up and sang some of their sacred songs for us, which were quite symphonious and pathetic, as they sing well. We will give an idea of the quaint wording of their sacred songs, such as—

> If you want to see the heavenly scene
> You must lay your head in Jordan's stream.
>
> *Chorus:*
> Ship of Zion, bear me over. Lord,
> I am bound to cross bold Jordan
> In dat mornin'.

Another was—

> Little Davy, play on your harp of a thousand strings.

Another—

> March on, dese bones er mine ;
> I am gwine to heaven
> In de mornin.

With others equally as original.

### "THE SUN DO SHOUT."

These same colored people declared to us that the sun rose up shouting every Christmas morning.

" How does it shout?" we asked.

" Oh, it jess jumps up an' down, up an' down, an' flutters as it never does any other mornin'."

" Ah, we guess it is all imagination on your part," we replied.

" Well, ef you don't bleve us, you jess look out for yourself next Christmas mornin'."

But we are digressing. We are not through with the pleasant visitors we met here. One we especially wish to mention, Mr. Wm. Whitehead, who was a general favorite, with his genial, pleasant way and witty good nature. Whenever he was present everybody felt in better humor with themselves and their neighbors. He was among the first to come and get cured of the rheumatism in his foot and ankle, and had no return of the trouble in three years, and when the second attack set in he came, and was cured again. Some of his good friends at Hillman said, while they did not want him to suffer, yet really they would like for him to have an excuse to come often. Colonel James Whitehead, his nephew, came, and was much benefited, while recovering from a spell of fever; and Dr. Whitehead, from Waynesboro, Ga., was cured of rheumatic gout on a recent visit to the Rock. It seems to run in the family of these good people to be clever, and prepossessing in appearance and kind in spirit. The Doctor gave the Rock due credit for curing his lame foot.

One of the most rapid cures we remember was that of Mr. Jake Allen, of Warrenton. He just came down to spend the day, he said; took his seat by the Rock, read his paper till dinner, went to dinner, came back, spent the afternoon, and, to his own great astonishment, rose out of his bed next morning sound and well of rheumatism, and no exposure since has brought on a recurrence.

Another gentleman, Mr. Seals, from Barnett, came for treatment as a last resort, for, said he, " I have tried nearly everything, and now I will try this." He said he had been to the water-cure establishment in Atlanta and spent a great deal of money without deriving any benefit. From the first day's treatment he commenced improving, and we never saw any one so proud of his final recovery.

Among other distinguished visitors to the rock was Rev. Dr. Spinning, of New York, who was broken completely down from arduous pastoral duties. His nerves were so shattered that his wife would not allow any correspondence to pass through his hands. In this condition he came to Hillman, accompanied by his wife, and in four or five weeks' treatment by the " Rock " he was sufficiently cured to return home, and was soon permanently well and filling his pulpit in his usual elegant style.

Just one other marvellous cure we will mention that was made here just a few days ago. A man was brought to the Rock in a buggy to be treated for rheumatism of a very severe kind, and was unable to walk. A week's treatment cured him, and now he is attending to his farm as usual. Many other cases I might mention, but I may as well do like Sam Weller, " drop off suddenly, to make 'em want to hear more."

# CHAPTER VII.

We visited some of the nearest towns or villages while sojourning at Hillman.

## CRAWFORDVILLE,

the county seat of Taliaferro county, is a place of some considerable note as being the home of the great Georgia statesman, Alexander H. Stephens. It is only eight miles from Hillman, on the Georgia railroad, with churches, schools, manufactories, a newspaper, &c. "Liberty Hall," the home of Mr. Stephens, is situated in the midst of this town. It is a pretty place, with large grounds and nicely laid-off walks. The large white residence, with its liberal and unusually wide halls and verandas, is of much interest to visitors. We were met and kindly shown through the house by Prof. Sanford, of the "Stephens High School." It was a common yet uncommon sight; the plain, common-place furniture standing as it stood the day Mr. Stephens died, in this inconspicuous room of so conspicuous a statesman.

On the bed was a plain white spread, with plain pillow and cases, all draped in mourning yet for the master of "Liberty Hall" and the master of superior statecraft; two small tables, on one of which still stands the drop-light, just as he left it; two antiquated desks, an old-fashioned wardrobe, old bureau and looking-glass, and a few steel engravings on the wall, pretty much completes the furniture of this memorial room. Alongside of his bed stands the small single bed of his faithful body-servant, Harry, who lifted him from bed to chair and from Liberty Hall to the halls of Congress, and among the last to lift him into the grave. It is said he was greatly attached to 'Harry, and when on reaching home from Congress he would often be met at the train by many of his warm-hearted friends, who insisted on lifting him from the car to the carriage, he would beg them to stand aside and let Harry lift him.

Harry was with him on his way to Atlanta to take the gubernatorial chair, and also a poor tramp who had come the night before to ask Mr. Stephens to get him a job. On seeing the tramp with the distinguished party, a gentleman asked Harry who that was they had along with them. "That's Marse Alec's tramp," said Harry. "Marse Alec is better to dogs than some men is to folks."

Everyone, in speaking of him to us, said he was the most generous and kind-hearted man they ever knew. Especially to young men just starting out in life would he lend a willing ear and helping hand. Mr. Stephens left Harry well provided for, with a good house and several acres of land, which we are told are now in the possession of Harry's widow.

As we passed out from Liberty Hall and walked down the wide, white walk that lead to the front entrance, we stopped and viewed, on the right of us, about midway from the house to the gate, the grave of this illustrious man. He has no monument yet, only a simple railing and two rows of brick surrounding the sacred mound, and on the mound a few sweet violets are growing.

We passed the old homestead of Mr. Stephens' father, who lies buried near the public road that leads from Hillman to Crawfordville.

WASHINGTON, GA.,

is eleven miles from Hillman, and is the terminus of the Washington branch of the Georgia railroad. It is an old and aristocratic town—said to be one hundred years old. It has about four thousand inhabitants, some of them very enterprising and moneyed people, who take great pride in keeping their city up with the modern improvements of the day, such as street-cars, electric-lights, telephones, &c. Colonel James A. Benson resides here, and is the owner of the Electric Mound Hotel and other valuable property at Hillman. He is engaged in an extensive mercantile business in this famous town, and also owns several farms in the adjacent counties. Being contiguous to Washington is a great addition to Hillman. The patients and visitors find it really a pleasant little trip going up on the 10 o'clock train and returning on the 5 o'clock train the same day. We frequently see them making these visits on pleasant days from Hillman to Washington. Sometimes they go shopping, or to visit the fine " Mary Willis " library, and sometimes to the theatre or ball. Washington is well known to have been the home of the late Robert Toombs, and this alone makes it of marked interest to the world. His residence is now owned by Colonel Frank H. Colley, a very prominent young lawyer, who married a Miss Toombs. He and his interesting family reside in this notable, grand old homestead.

Of Robert Toombs, the invincible; the brilliant orator and proud statesman; of noble birth and lordly mien; a tower of strength and strong will in the heyday of his life; soft and tender of heart in his declining years, much has been said. And everything connected with him seems of unusual interest. Even the reminiscences of an old gray-haired colored man whom we saw at Hillman was of much interest. We asked if he knew General Toombs. " Did I know Marse Robert Toombs? 'Deed I did; 'pears to me I see him now, coming down the road wid two great big horses hitched to his buggy, gwine on down to Baker county, whar he owned 'bout three thousand acres o' land. When he was coming on back something broke 'bout his buggy. I was standing close by de road in de cotton field, an' I seed the buggy stop, an' I runned up an fixed it all right. Den I seed him put his hand in his pocket, and I thought he was going to give me fifty cents, but, my Lord! he took out a five-dollar note and flung it at me, an' 'fore I knowed it dem horses had dashed off wid him 'fore I could say 'thankee, sar.' Ah, Lord! he was de richest man anywheres 'bout here. He kept his waitman George dressed as fine as Marse Robert hissef, an' a gold watch on same as hisen. He gin his cook 'oman a house an' lot, too, 'fore he died. He was mighty good whar he took a liken, an' he was rich ernuff to do jess like he please. Many a time is I been herd de train whoop fore de regular time for it to come out, an' I used to look out to see who was in it, an' dar wouldn't be a blessed soul in dar but Marse Robert, an he was gwine on to Atlanta or Augusta, one or tother. Den I said, Yas, he got so much money he done spen dat fifty dollars for de extra train to take him out to Barnett, so he can make room to put down another fifty dollars."

The noble citizens of Washington, Georgia, ordered a monument from Italy, which was shipwrecked on the ocean and lost. They ordered another, which arrived safely, and was erected over his grave in the pretty little cemetery of his native city.

SHARON, GEORGIA,

is a small, pretty town, three miles from Hillman, on the Washington branch of the Georgia railroad. Here live several well-to-do merchants. Among the wealthiest we count Messrs Edward Croke,

James Kendrick, and L. A. Moore. The people are quite progressive and literary, with several good schools and churches. The Catholic church and convent are handsome buildings.

Sharon is quite an emporium for cotton, and we often see the long depot ladened with bales ready for shipping during cotton-picking time, which continues from August until the last of December.

"Ah! cotton-picking time in Georgia!" What a happy time it is for the picker. What pictures crowd his fond imagination of the good time to follow the picking of "dat cotton." How independent and happy the picker looks in the snowy fields. How gaily he sings as he snatches the fleecy staple from the bolls to the basket, and from the basket to the barn, to be bound into bales. Then the bales are bought, and the greenbacks abound.

Somebody has said "Cotton is king." The author of that trite old saying might reverse it, and say "*Cotton* has many *kings*."

### RAYTOWN, GA.,

is in five miles of Hillman, with a goodly number of inhabitants and several stores. It has some old landmarks of good and noble families who have passed " over the river." Among them was an uncle of Alexander H. Stephens—Mr. Grier, the founder of the well-known "Grier Almanac." People who remember him say he greatly assisted and encouraged his nephew (Mr. Stephens) on his first launching out in life as a young lawyer.

### · BARNETT, GA.

This little station and town on the Georgia railroad, between Augusta and Atlanta, is about seven miles from Hillman, and has a tel-

53

egraph office (as also Sharon, Ga.), stores, and depot. Passengers from Augusta, Atlanta, and other points get off at this station and take the Washington branch of the Georgia railroad for Sharon, Hillman, and Washington.

FICKLIN, GA.,

another station worthy of mention, is three miles from Hillman, on the Washington branch of the Georgia railroad.

SANDY CROSS

is a little over a mile from Hillman, on the west end of Mr. Hillman's plantation. It is called " Sandy Cross" on account of two public roads crossing there. It is a pretty place and quite a village, with several buildings and fine water, and admirably arranged to build or start a town. Dr. J. A. Rhodes, a prominent young physician, resides here and may be considered a resident physician of Hillman.

SOCIAL HALL

is the family homestead of the Hillmans. Rev. Joseph Hillman, father of Rev. A. L. Hillman, lived and died in this house. It is a large two-story building, with ten or twelve rooms, with large verandas. It is not quite a mile from the Electric Rock, and is now rented for the year by Mr. William L. Jackson for a boarding-house.

There is another boarding-house at Hillman, owned by Mrs. Jennie Sims, within a few hundred yards of the Electric Rock.

Rev. A. L. Hillman and family live about a mile from the Electric Rock, on a high knoll, nearly covered with white flint rocks and pebbles. These, with the pine and oak grove and other pretty surroundings, give his place a picturesque appearance.

## MOUNT MONTEIRO

is the name of a beautiful elevation near the Electric Rock. It is a magnificent site for a hotel, commanding as it does so many fine views of the surrounding country, with hills and dales, roads and residences, out in the distance, and well-wooded with pines and oaks intermingled over this pretty little mount. Monteiro, when interpreted, means "Sacred Mountain."

## BUYING LOTS.

In riding over this remarkable place we saw many desirable spots to build on, and it occurred to us what an inducement it must be to make a home here and derive the benefits of the fine mineral waters combined with the virtue of the Electric Rock. When the world becomes fully aware of its great worth, no doubt Hillman will be rapidly populated. Various parties have already bought lots; some have built and made their homes here; while others have availed themselves of the opportunity to speculate. We selected a very pretty site and will locate here, and will always be glad to see our genial friends whom we have met at this Mecca of America, where standeth in greatness and grandeur the "Rocks that Shock."

May not Edison, the world-renowned scientist, probe deep into these mysterious batteries of Nature and solve, if possible, their hidden virtues?

# PRESTON BELVIN,

## FINE ART

## FURNITURE,

### No. 18 GOVERNOR STREET.

Sole Agent for the Richmond Cedar Works' Celebrated MOTH-PROOF RED
CEDAR CHEST.

# A. HOEN & CO.,

# LITHOGRAPHERS

——AND——

# ENGRAVERS.

## RICHMOND, - - VIRGINIA.

# ISAAC S. TOWER,

### GENERAL AGENT FOR THE SALE OF

# The Oliver Chilled Plows,

THE STUDEBAKER WAGONS AND ROAD CARTS,

THE CHAMPION HARVESTING MACHINES,

"TIGER," TAYLOR," and "LONE STAR" RAKES.

Orders solicited for all kinds of Implements for the Farm.

**No. 1528 E. MAIN STREET (P. O. Box 444), RICHMOND, VA.**

---

# J. W. FERGUSSON & SON,

 PRINTERS

*6-8-10 Fourteenth Street, - - Richmond, Va.*

ESTIMATES ON ANY CHARACTER OF WORK GIVEN.

---

# B. F. SMITH

### DEALER IN

*Hall's Safe and Lock Company's Standard Fire and Burglar-Proof Safes, Time and Combination Locks, Bank Vaults, Bank Furniture, and Wire Work.*

AGENCY OF BUFFALO SCALE COMPANY'S STANDARD SCALES.

**No. 28 North Ninth Street, Richmond, Va.**

---

# G. W. DAVIS,

## Photographer,

## 827 Broad Street,

Superior Work—Moderate Prices.

## Richmond, Va.

CPSIA information can be obtained
at www.ICGtesting.com
Printed in the USA
BVOW08s1718181117

500715BV00006B/58/P